Acting Edition

I0591993

The Fisherman and His Wife

by Ruth Newton

ISBN 978-0-573-65222-6

www.concordtheatricals.com
www.concordtheatricals.co.uk

No one shall make any changes in this title(s) for the purpose of production. No part of this book may be reproduced, stored in a retrieval system, scanned, uploaded, or transmitted in any form, by any means, now known or yet to be invented, including mechanical, electronic, digital, photocopying, recording, videotaping, or otherwise, without the prior written permission of the publisher. No one shall share this title(s), or any part of this title(s), through any social media or file hosting websites.

For all inquiries regarding motion picture, television, online/digital and other media rights, please contact Concord Theatricals Corp.

MUSIC AND THIRD-PARTY MATERIALS USE NOTE

Licensees are solely responsible for obtaining formal written permission from copyright owners to use copyrighted music and/or other copyrighted third-party materials (e.g., artworks, logos) in the performance of this play and are strongly cautioned to do so. If no such permission is obtained by the licensee, then the licensee must use only original music and materials that the licensee owns and controls. Licensees are solely responsible and liable for clearances of all third-party copyrighted materials, including without limitation music, and shall indemnify the copyright owners of the play(s) and their licensing agent, Concord Theatricals Corp., against any costs, expenses, losses and liabilities arising from the use of such copyrighted third-party materials by licensees. For music, please contact the appropriate music licensing authority in your territory for the rights to any incidental music.

IMPORTANT BILLING AND CREDIT REQUIREMENTS

If you have obtained performance rights to this title, please refer to your licensing agreement for important billing and credit requirements.

NOTE ON THE SETS FOR THE PLAY

The sets for THE FISHERMAN AND HIS WIFE need not be elaborate. One upstage drop will serve as background for all the changes; it then becomes the US. wall in the castle. The opening hovel set should be very simple. An US. wall, a well-braced doorframe D.L., a suspended window US. of the door, and a suggested wall at the R. The US. wall, when reversed, can become the cottage facade, placed well US. If possible, banners and shields should be added for the castle scene.

It is suggested, for safety's sake, that the lip of the stage be well marked with luminous tape or paint.

3

The Fisherman and His Wife

*The houselights fade, and in the darkness, we hear a
soft humming of voices.*
*A front spotlight fades up on MR. FISHERMAN.
Seated on the lip of the stage, holding a fishing rod
in his hands, he is fast asleep and snoring. His line
extends into the orchestra pit.*
*The offstage humming grows louder, then it abruptly
ceases.*

MR. FISHERMAN. (*startled awake*) I'm up! I'm up! (*He
comes to.*) Well, what do you know? I must have dozed
off. (*He notices the audience.*) Oh, hi! Know what I'm
doing? Right! Fishing. Ever go fishing? You did? Catch
anything? How big. Wow! I hope I catch one that
big—or I'll be afraid to go home. Know why? My wife.
My wife, Nancy. That's why. See, if I don't catch a fish,
we won't have anything to eat. And Nancy doesn't like
to go hungry. No, sir. Being hungry makes her MEAN!
You ever been hungry? You have! Well, did it make you
mean? (*There is a tugging on his line.*) Oh, oh. Can't
talk now. Got a bite!

(*His rod is almost bent double. Suddenly, out of the
orchestra pit, an enormous, golden FISH leaps,
shaking and quivering in the light. The fishing line
is attached to its mouth.*)

Look at that! Biggest fish I ever saw! Oh, no you don't,
my big beauty—you're not going to get away from me!

(*MR. FISHERMAN is now on his feet, playing the FISH quite skillfully. The FISH leaves the pit and races up the aisle, pleading with the audience to help him. Followspot, if available, stays on him.*)

THE FISH. Help me! Please help me! Oh, can't somebody help me?

MR. FISHERMAN. (*simultaneously*) Don't help him. Don't touch my fish! Why, a fish that size will feed Nancy and me for weeks. Fried fish . . . baked fish . . . broiled fish . . . fish cakes . . . fish chowder . . . fish balls . . . dried fish—and a little left over for the cat. (*He reels the FISH back down the aisle to the stage apron.*) I've never seen a fish like that in my life. (*to audience*) Have you?

(*He leans over, preparing to haul in his catch—when suddenly, the FISH leaps up onto the stage, knocking the old man flat. But he hangs onto the rod as the FISH dances back and forth, trying desperately to get free.*)

MR. FISHERMAN. (*still on the ground*) I'm plumb tuckered out. What a beauty! (*He gets up.*) Wait till Nancy sees this! (*Suddenly the FISH collapses, lies fluttering, breathless.*) That's better. Now, let's have a look at you. (*MR. FISHERMAN moves closer to it. The FISH is trying to speak. To audience.*) He's trying to say something! Aw, come on, fish can't talk! (*He bends over to listen. The FISH is trying to speak. To audience.*) Do you believe fish can talk? (*They do.*) Well, what's he trying to say? (*to FISH*) What did you say?

FISH. (*gasping*) Put me back. Please . . . put . . . me
. . . back . . . in the sea.

MR. FISHERMAN. Put you back! (*to audience*) He
wants me to put him back in the sea! (*to FISH*) No way.
You're coming home with me — and ZIP! right into the
frying pan — where all good fish belong.

FISH. I'm not a fish.

MR. FISHERMAN. What?

FISH. I said, I'm not a fish.

MR. FISHERMAN. Not a fish! (*to audience*) He says
he's not a fish. Do you believe that?

FISH. Please, sir . . . I beg you — put me back in the
water. I can't live out of the sea.

MR. FISHERMAN. Well, now wait just a minute here. If
you're not a fish, what are you?

FISH. Put me back. Please, put me back. And then I'll
tell you. Please! I can't breathe!

MR. FISHERMAN. Poor thing. (*to audience*) What
should I do? I feel sorry for the poor creature. And be-
sides . . . a fish who can talk . . . What do you think?
Shall I put him back in the water?

(*The audience says yes.*)

MR. FISHERMAN. Oh, boy . . . I'll never hear the end
of this. When I get home my wife Nancy will beat me,
berate me, bean me with a stool. She'll banish me for-
ever.

FISH. Please . . .

MR. FISHERMAN. If I put you back, you won't run
away, will you?

FISH. No, I won't.

MR. FISHERMAN. Promise?

FISH. (*gasping*) Promise.

MR. FISHERMAN. (*to audience*) Should I believe him?

(*Audience says yes.*)

All right. Here we go. (*He starts helping the FISH back into the sea. Then, he stops.*) Look, I'm going to leave the hook in your mouth. So if you're playing a trick on me, I'll just have to reel you back in. All right?

FISH. Yes. Hurry. Please. (*The FISH is now in the water. He does a frolicking dance of joy all up and down the aisle. MR. FISHERMAN watches.*)

MR. FISHERMAN. Isn't that the prettiest sight you ever saw? I'm glad I let him go. But what am I going to tell my wife? She's never going to believe this fish story.

FISH. (*now at rim of stage*) Thank you. Thank you. Thank you! It's good to be alive! (*FISH takes a big, shimmering hook—which he has palmed—out of his mouth. He hands it to MR. FISHERMAN.*) Here. I want you to have this.

MR. FISHERMAN. (*looks at it*) That's not my hook, Fish.

FISH. I know.

MR. FISHERMAN. This hook is gold! Is it real gold?

FISH. Yes. And it's a magic fish-hook.

MR. FISHERMAN. Magic!

FISH. Yes. If ever you need anything . . . cast it in the water . . . and I'll come to you.

MR. FISHERMAN. Go on! Magic! There's no such thing. (*to audience*) Now even the fish are telling fish stories.

FISH. I told you, sir—I am not a fish.

MR. FISHERMAN. (*scoffs*) Not a fish! Then what are

you – a goldsmith . . . an alchemist . . . a creature of my imagination? What are you?

FISH. (*in a strange, far-away voice*) I am a royal prince, doomed to spend my life in the sea. An evil witch has cast a spell on me . . . and never again shall I roam the land . . . or breathe the air of other men . . . Farewell . . . Farewell . . .

MR. FISHERMAN. Come back! Come back! He's gone. And look at me: All I have to show for my day's work is a fish-hook. (*He gathers up his things.*) What am I going to tell my poor wife? (*to audience*) Listen, you saw him, didn't you? I didn't dream it, or make it up, did I? How could I have dreamed it. Here's the fish-hook, right here in my hand. All right! (*He starts off* R., *then stops.*) Listen – if my wife Nancy asks you about this, you'll tell her it's all true, won't you? Thanks. (*He exits* R.)

(*The traveller curtain opens part way. We see a small hovel. The furniture is sparse, broken and badly mended. This is obviously the little house of MR. FISHERMAN and his wife, NANCY. NANCY is hammering a nail into the door frame to hold up what passes for curtains. She restores the rod that holds the curtains, moves back to admire her work.*)

MRS. FISHERMAN. There! That's fixed. Now what's next? This whole place is falling down.

(*She backs up and accidentally tumbles onto the cot, which collapses, and over she goes, legs and petticoats flying into the air. The audience laughs.*)

NANCY. (*sitting up*) Oh, you think it's funny, do you?

Well, I don't. There's nothing in this place that isn't worn out, ugly or busted. I'm sick of it. Sick, sick, sick of being poor. Oh, oh — I hear someone coming.

(*MRS. TRIPPETT and MRS. FOLLOWELL enter* L. *They are much better dressed than MRS. FISHERMAN. MRS. TRIPPETT carries a small basket covered with a red checked cloth.*)

MRS. TRIPPETT. (*entering*) . . . so I said to him, "Norman Trippett," I said, "I'm going on a mercy of mission . . ."

MRS. FOLLOWELL. . . . mission of mercy . . .

MRS. TRIPPETT. (*irked*) . . . yes . . . and I said, "Not even your bellyache is going to stop me." My dear, you should have heard him!

MRS. FOLLOWELL. What did he say?

MRS. TRIPPETT. What could he say? (*looks at the FISHERMAN's house*) There it is. That's the little shack. Isn't it awful?

MRS. FOLLOWELL. Disgraceful. How can people live like that? (*Inside the house, MRS. FISHERMAN hears them.*)

MRS. FISHERMAN. I'm not going to let them in. I'll hide so they'll think there's no one at home. (*She hides — then pops up again to speak to audience.*) You won't tell them where I am, will you? Promise? (*She hides.*)

(*MRS. TRIPPETT and MRS. FOLLOWELL have reached the doorstep. MRS. TRIPPETT knocks. No answer.*)

MRS. TRIPPETT. Mrs. Fisherman! Yoo-hoo, anybody home? Mrs. Fisherman, I've brought you a basketful of goodies! (*to MRS. FOLLOWELL*) How odd. She never goes out. Peek in the window, Mrs. Followell—see if you can see anything.

MRS. FOLLOWELL. (*doing so*) Not a soul. My gracious, what a sorry little house. I'd heard they were poor—but —my goodness. (*She comes back down.*) Is the door locked?

(*MRS. FISHERMAN, hearing this, oozes across the stage and crawls up against the door. MRS. TRIP-PETT rattles and pushes at the door, jouncing MRS. FISHERMAN, but she can't get in.*)

MRS. TRIPPETT. (*giving up*) Well! All that long trip out here—for nothing.

MRS. FOLLOWELL. What a shame. Why don't you just leave the basket on the step?

MRS. TRIPPETT. Don't be stupid. That way they wouldn't even know whom to thank.

MRS. FOLLOWELL. Oh, of course. Well, couldn't you leave a note? With your name on it?

MRS. TRIPPETT. Better still—I'll come back tomorrow —to pick up my basket and tablecloth. That way I can see how much they appreciate my generosity. Come along, Mrs. Followell. (*They start off.*) Wait just a moment. (*to audience*) Do you know where they are?

(*The audience responds, but MRS. TRIPPETT will not hear any of them who tell her where MRS. FISH-ERMAN is. MRS. FISHERMAN, of course, is waving at them to keep them from revealing her presence.*)

MRS. TRIPPETT. Hmmmm. It's all very odd. Well . . .

come along, Mrs. Followell. Let's be off. (*They exit* L., *chattering.*)

MRS. FISHERMAN. (*whispers to audience*) Have they gone? (*She opens the door and peeks out. She picks up the basket and looks in it as she walks* DS.) Terrible women. Mission of mercy! If you squeezed the last drop of charity out of both of them you wouldn't get enough to rinse out the eye of a butterfly. Look at this: half a chicken, picked over . . . rotten tomatoes . . . stale bread — left-overs. Charity! Here's what I think of their charity!

(*She winds up the basket and throws it off* R. *MR. FISHERMAN, off* R., *yells. He enters, his face swathed in the checkered cloth. The dead chicken hangs around his neck, and he carries the bread.*)

MR. FISHERMAN. Hey! What is this! (*He struggles to get the cloth off his face, looks at the food.*) Nancy! Throwing good food away?

MRS. FISHERMAN. Good food!? Trash! Garbage! And it's high time you got back. You've been gone for hours, probably dawdling and day-dreaming. (*She goes into the house.*) Where's the fish you caught? Bring it here so I can cook it and we can have a decent supper.

MR. FISHERMAN. (*to audience*) Did you tell her I caught a fish? Then how did she find out? Well, I'd better go in and face the music. (*He enters the house, puts the bread, cloth and chicken on the table; stashes the fishing rod near the door; hangs his hat on a peg. MRS. FISHERMAN bangs some dishes onto the table.*)

MRS. FISHERMAN. Well, where's the fish?

MR. FISHERMAN. Got away.

MRS. FISHERMAN. What?

MR. FISHERMAN. I said he got away.

MRS. FISHERMAN. (*sits at table*) What do you mean "he"? A fish is an it — not a "he". Come eat. Give thanks for this stale bread . . . amen.

MR. FISHERMAN. (*sits at table*) This one was a he. And he . . . ah . . . well, he told me . . . he said that he was an enchanted prince — that some wicked witch had cast a spell on him.

MRS. FISHERMAN. Andrew Fisherman, you've been drinking!

MR. FISHERMAN. Nancy Fisherman, I have not. Here. (*He shows her the golden fish-hook.*) Ever seen a fish-hook like that?

MRS. FISHERMAN. (*looking at it*) It's gold! Andy! It's solid gold. We can sell it!

MR. FISHERMAN. No, we can't.

MRS. FISHERMAN. What do you mean, no we can't. Why not? (*She puts a crust of the bread in her mouth, spits it out immediately.*) Put a decent meal in our bellies for a change.

MR. FISHERMAN. We can't sell it, Nancy.

MRS. FISHERMAN. We're going to sell it, Andrew. I'm sick of being poor and hungry. Sick of this shack we're living in. Sick of other people's charity.

MR. FISHERMAN. Nancy, listen to me. The fish said he was an enchanted prince, and that this fish-hook is magical. (*He takes it from her.*) And he said that if ever I needed anything . . .

MRS. FISHERMAN. The fish talked? (*He nods.*) You sure you didn't stop off with the boys and have a few beers. (*He nods.*) He said that's a magic fish-hook? (*He nods.*) And you didn't ask him for anything?

MR. FISHERMAN. Well . . . he *gave* me the hook, Nancy.

MRS. FISHERMAN. Honestly! I don't know why God put a head on your shoulders. There's certainly nothing stored inside it. Go back. Right now. Bait this hook and catch that fish again. Tell him what we want: a nice little white cottage . . . geraniums growing in window-boxes . . . carpets and furniture . . . a nice little vegetable garden . . . oh, yes, and a cow, for milk. Plus . . . a little money wouldn't hurt, long as you're asking.

MR. FISHERMAN. Nancy . . . If you could have seen him . . .

MRS. FISHERMAN. I see *us!* Now go on.

MR. FISHERMAN. But, Nancy, I . . .

MRS. FISHERMAN. Andrew, don't argue. Go!

(*MR. FISHERMAN reluctantly gets up, gets his fishing gear, clamps his hat on his head. He comes back to the table, glowering at MRS. FISHERMAN, stuffs a crust of bread in his pocket and exits* R. *The lights fade on the house, and the curtain closes. MR. FISHERMAN enters* R., *in front of the curtain. The lighting suggests night.*)

MR. FISHERMAN. Plague take the woman! A pox on her! Now blast my hide, I don't want to do it. (*to audience*) Did you ever have to do something you didn't want to do? (*They answer.*) Not much fun, is it? What do you think I should do? Catch the fish again! But that's just what I don't want to do! Still . . . come to think of it, a little white cottage with red geraniums at the windows would be nice, wouldn't it. The other question is: what happens if I *don't* do it? There'll be no living with her. Well, might as well give it a try. (*While talking, he has tied the golden hook to his line. He now tosses it into the "water."*)

MR. FISHERMAN. (*sings in a croaking voice*)
Fishie, fishie in the sea
Take this hook and come to me.
For Mistress Nancy, my darling wife,
The joy and burden of my life,
Has a favor to ask of thee.
(*to audience*) Now if that isn't the stupidest thing! A grown man standing out here, baying at the moon like a lonesome hound-dog.

(*He stops and listens. Once again, we hear the mysterious humming offstage. MR. FISHERMAN is a bit frightened by it and doesn't want to show it. The humming ceases abruptly — and the FISH appears.*)

FISH. Old man . . . old man . . . I heard you calling me. But I was a long, long way . . . under the sea. What is it?

MR. FISHERMAN. Oh, am I glad to see you! I was beginning to think I'd made you up. (*He reels in the golden fish-hook.*) Look, Prince, I don't know how to tell you this. My wife Nancy — Oh, shoot! This is embarrassing.

FISH. What are you trying to say?

MR. FISHERMAN. (*to audience*) Help me out, will you? Tell him what my wife wants. (*They do.*)

FISH. A small, white cottage . . . red geraniums . . . a garden . . . carpets and furniture . . . and a cow.

MR. FISHERMAN. That's it — oh, yes — and a little money in the old sock, if that's all right with you.

FISH. Go home, old man . . . and see what you find.

(*FISH disappears. From behind the curtain: An old time square-dance is in progress. There are fiddlers and a caller. As the curtain goes out — to a wider opening this time — MR. FISHERMAN is engulfed in a celebration. It is taking place in the garden of a lovely little white cottage. Someone takes MR. FISHERMAN's rod and reel, and he is whisked off to join the figures of the dance. MRS. FISHERMAN walks proudly around the dancers. She is beaming, encouraging everyone to enjoy her hospitality. Those who are not dancing are eating or drinking — or gossiping. MRS. TRIPPETT and MRS. FOLLOWELL, DS.L., are green with envy. They look on with disdain, not taking part. When the dance ends, MRS. FISHERMAN moves down to them.*)

MRS. FISHERMAN. I hope you ladies are enjoying yourselves.

MRS. TRIPPETT and MRS. FOLLOWELL. (*simultaneously*) Oh, yes, indeed. Indeed we are. Lovely party. Lovely house. (*MRS. TRIPPETT turns her back on MRS. FISHERMAN, and as if continuing her conversation, snubs her.*)

MRS. TRIPPETT. So, as I was telling you — next week we're moving into the mansion. My dear, 26 bedrooms . . . 26 — no, *28* bathrooms . . . servants . . . wine cellar . . . and a dining hall as big as a skating rink. I haven't even *found* the kitchen . . . (*MRS. FISHERMAN moves away, furious. The musicians begin to play again, and the caller announces another reel.*)

MRS. FISHERMAN. No! That's it. The party is over! Everybody out! Go home! All of you! Out! Out! Out! (*This is to MRS. TRIPPETT and MRS. FOLLOWELL, whom she shoos out of the garden.*) Everybody out! (*The dancers, musicians and guest, protesting, disappear.*)

MR. FISHERMAN. Nancy—what are you doing?

MRS. FISHERMAN. It's time for everyone to go home. The party's over.

MR. FISHERMAN. Why?! We were having a wonderful time. The house is beautiful . . . and I love the garden. Nancy! You're crying! What is it?

MRS. FISHERMAN. I'm not crying! I'm angry! Andrew, I want you to go back. Go back to that fish. Tell him you want a great castle . . . with hundreds of rooms, hundreds of bathrooms . . . and hundreds of servants . . . and horses and grooms, and a moat with a draw-bridge. And I want silks and satins and jewelry and lords and ladies . . .

MR. FISHERMAN. I won't do it.

MRS. FISHERMAN. And an army of guards and sol-diers—What did you say?!

MR. FISHERMAN. I said I won't do it.

MRS. FISHERMAN. You will.

MR. FISHERMAN. I won't. This little cottage is perfect for us—more than I ever dreamed of having. I will not ask for anything more.

MRS. FISHERMAN. You will.

MR. FISHERMAN. I won't.

MRS. FISHERMAN. Then you'll live here alone. I'll not stay another moment.

MR. FISHERMAN. Nancy!

MRS. FISHERMAN. Andrew! (*There is a long hostile silence. Finally:*)

MR. FISHERMAN. Nancy . . .

MRS. FISHERMAN. What.

MR. FISHERMAN. I'll make a bargain with you.

MRS. FISHERMAN. What?

MR. FISHERMAN. Let's ask them. (*He points to the au-dience.*) No matter what they say, I'll abide by it. Agreed?

MRS. FISHERMAN. (*She hands him his fishing rod.*) Of course, I'll agree. (*She knows she's won.*)

(*They walk* DS. *and address the audience. Curtain closes.*)

MR. FISHERMAN. Should I ask the fish for a castle?
MRS. FISHERMAN. Say yes! Say yes!

(*There may be a little discussion on this point, as each of them persuades the audience to take sides. Once the question is settled, the lights fade. MRS. FISHERMAN exits* L., *and MR. FISHERMAN, now in the spotlight, moves to* C., *and casts his line in the water.*)

MR. FISHERMAN. (*sings*)
Fishie, fishie in the sea,
Wherever you are — don't come to me!
For Mistress Nancy, my greedy spouse,
Not content with hovel or house,
Now wants another favor of thee.
(*He closes his eyes and crosses his fingers.*)
(*to audience*) Close your eyes and cross your fingers, everyone. Maybe the fish won't come. Help me! Come on, all of you! Help me. (*The mysterious humming begins offstage.*) Put your fingers in your ears! Don't listen to it! Maybe it'll go away. (*The humming grows louder. His eyes still closed, his ears stopped with his fingers.*) You're not helping! I can still hear it! Go away . . . no more fish today . . . no more fishes . . . no more wishes.

(*The music stops abruptly. The audience will probably*

tell him that FISH has appeared. He pretends not to hear them.)

FISH. What is it, old man? (*Fish reaches up and pulls at the fishing line.*)

MR. FISHERMAN. (*opens his eyes, unstops his ears*) Oh . . . you're here.

FISH. Of course. What is it you want?

MR. FISHERMAN. I'm too embarrassed to tell you.

FISH. Go ahead. Nothing surprises me.

MR. FISHERMAN. Well, this might. First, I love the cottage. Thank you very much.

FISH. But. . . ?

MR. FISHERMAN. Well . . . you see . . . my wife Nancy . . .

FISH. Wants something better.

MR. FISHERMAN. Right!

FISH. Bigger and better.

MR. FISHERMAN. That's right! That's right! How did you know?

FISH. And what do you want?

MR. FISHERMAN. Me?

FISH. You.

MR. FISHERMAN. What do I want? Aw . . . it's not a question of me and what I want.

FISH. Are you sure?

MR. FISHERMAN. Well . . . (*angrily*) Well, of course I'm sure! All I want is to make my wife happy . . .

FISH. And living in a castle will do that? I once lived in a castle . . . Never mind. Go home, old man, and see what you find.

(*Fish disappears. The lights fade. The curtain goes out. And the lights come up on a magnificent great hall in a castle. MR. FISHERMAN enters from where he was C., and moves DS.L. The dancers, masked, now wear capes of gold, bits of ribbon, tiaras, jewelry. They are dancing a stately court dance. There is a strange silence throughout the dance; movement and lighting give it an unreal, dream-like quality. The music is formal and strict, but filled with dissonant harmonies. At the climax of the dance, the dancers form two lines diagonally from U.R. to D.L. MRS. FISHERMAN, gaudily arrayed and bejeweled, walks through the lines and down to MR. FISHERMAN. Her mask is the most elaborate of them all; there is a coldness and immobility about the features that is nightmarish in feeling. The dancers bow low to her as she passes.*)

MRS. FISHERMAN. And now, husband . . . one last request.

MR. FISHERMAN. (*not sure it's she*) Nancy?

MRS. FISHERMAN. Go back to the fish. And tell him this for me. (*She clasps him by the shoulders, forcing him to his knees. She leans over him and whispers something in his ear. He protests. But he cannot get away.*)

MR. FISHERMAN. I won't.

MRS. FISHERMAN. You will. (*She bends him back and forth like a rag doll.*)

MR. FISHERMAN. (*terrified*) I won't! (*MRS. FISHERMAN lets him fall. She turns to the dancers and gestures imperiously.*)

MRS. FISHERMAN. Take him!

(*Under STROBE lighting, the dancers drag MR. FISHERMAN U.C., surround him, maul him, toss him up in the air, catch him, toss him up again. MR.*

FISHERMAN yells each time he flies into the air. Then, he is put down on the lip of the stage. Someone hands him his fishing rod. The dancers now move us., striking grotesque, threatening poses, with MRS. FISHERMAN dominant. The STROBE goes out. The curtain closes. The spotlight comes up on MR. FISHERMAN. He stands with his back to the audience, his arms spread out against the curtain as though to keep the nightmare from spilling out into the house.)

MR. FISHERMAN. No! No! Nooooo! (*He turns.*) What am I going to do? What am I going to do. (*to audience*) You know what she wants now? (*They will probably tell him.*) Right! She wants to be the Queen — no, not the Queen! She wants to be the Empress! She wants to be the Empress of the whole blasted world! What am I going to do? Shall I tell the fish? (*They will probably say yes.*) You think I should? Well, I don't want to. And I won't! (*He sits and sings, sadly. And as he sings, without being aware of it, he lets his fishing line down into the pit.*)

Fishie . . . fishie . . . in the sea,

Stay away — far away from me.

For my Nancy, I find,

Is losing her mind.

(*spoken*) She now wants to be the Empress of the world!

(*There is no humming. Only a long silence. And then:*)

FISH. (*unseen*) Go home, old man, and see what you find!

(*FISH's voice — on tape — now comes from several different directions, repeating and echoing the above line. During this, MR. FISHERMAN takes exactly*

*the same position as he held at the opening of the
show. He is sleeping and snoring. And when the
sound stops:*)

MR. FISHERMAN. (*waking*) I'm up! I'm up! Well, what
do you know! I must have dozed off. "Go home, old
man, and see what you find . . ." Go home . . . go home
. . . (*He rises.*) Go home, old man, and see what you
find. The Empress Fishwife, that's what I'll find.

(*He puts his rod over his shoulder. He does not realize
it, but there is a nice, big fish on it. If the audience
tells him, he doesn't hear them. He exits* R., *muttering to himself. When the curtain opens, we are back
in the hovel. However, it looks more cheerful.
There is a bright spread on the cot, a pretty cloth on
the table, as well as a vase of fresh flowers. MRS.
FISHERMAN is in a pretty frock. And she has
guests — MRS. TRIPPETT and MRS. FOLLO-
WELL. A picnic basket, covered with a red checked
cloth sits by the table. As the lights go up, all three
women are laughing. It is obvious that they like and
enjoy each other.*)

MRS. TRIPPETT. Oh, it was so funny! Everytime I
think about it, I laugh till I cry. (*She wipes her eyes with
a handkerchief.*)
MRS. FOLLOWELL. Me, too! (*She wipes her eyes also.
All three of them burst into laughter again.*)
MR. FISHERMAN. (*MR. FISHERMAN enters* R., *still
muttering to himself.*) Go home and see what you find
. . . go home to the Empress of the whole blasted world
. . . (*He crosses the stage and turns to open the door.
Suddenly he realizes what has happened. He jumps*

back, races down c. *and addresses the audience.*) Do you see what I see? What happened? What's going on here!? I'd better go in and find out. (*He enters the house. Gruffly.*) Ladies . . . (*He hangs up his hat by the door, the rod still over his shoulder.*)

MRS. FISHERMAN. Hello, dear. Catch anything?

MR. FISHERMAN. No.

MRS. FISHERMAN. (*rises and goes to him*) Then what is this? (*shows him the fish on his line*)

MR. FISHERMAN. (*puzzled*) Now where in tarnation did that come from?

MRS. FISHERMAN. (*laughs*) The ocean, I imagine. (*She removes the fish and shows it to the women; she then puts it in an ice-box or cooler.*)

MRS. TRIPPETT. (*looking at fish*) My, isn't that a beauty!

MRS. FOLLOWELL. My, yes! (*MR. FISHERMAN is stunned.*)

MRS. FISHERMAN. (*returning to table*) Come say hello, dear. Mrs. Trippett and Mrs. Followell were going on a picnic—and they stopped by to see if we'd like to join them.

MRS. TRIPPETT. I hope you will. We've brought enough food for an army.

MR. FISHERMAN. Nancy, could I talk to you for a minute.

MRS. FISHERMAN. Why, of course, dear. Excuse me, ladies. (*She crosses down to him.*) What is it, Andy?

MR. FISHERMAN. What's going on here?

MRS. FISHERMAN. What do you mean?

MR. FISHERMAN. (*whispering*) What happened to the castle?

MRS. FISHERMAN. What?

MR. FISHERMAN. I said what happened to the castle?

MRS. FISHERMAN. (*very loud*) The castle?

MR. FISHERMAN. (*shushing her*) Yes, the castle. Where is it?

MRS. FISHERMAN. What castle? What are you talking about. (*She feels his forehead.*) Andy—are you feeling all right?

MR. FISHERMAN. (*brushing her hand away*) Of course I'm feeling all right. Come outside for a minute, will you?

MRS. FISHERMAN. (*demurring*) Andrew . . .

MR. FISHERMAN. (*taking her hand*) Come outside. (*He opens the door and pulls her outside.*)

MRS. FISHERMAN. What is the matter with you? (*to the women*) We'll be right back. (*as he pulls her* DS.) Andy, we have guests. . . !

(*The lights dim on the interior of the house. The two of them are now* DS. *in the spotlight.*)

MR. FISHERMAN. Where have you been all day?

MRS. FISHERMAN. Right here! Why?

MR. FISHERMAN. And you didn't see a castle—or even a cottage? You didn't give a big party . . . with food and dancing . . .

MRS. FISHERMAN. (*starts for house*) I'm going to call the doctor. You've had too much sun!

MR. FISHERMAN. Nancy, come back here! (*She does.*) You didn't tell me that you wanted a little white cottage . . . and then you wanted a big castle . . . and then—

MRS. FISHERMAN. I don't know what you're talking about. I haven't seen you since you left the house early this morning to go fishing. (*looks at him quizically*) You haven't been nipping at the bottle, have you?

MR. FISHERMAN. No, I have not been nipping at the bottle. That's exactly what you asked me when I came home and told you about the fish!

MRS. FISHERMAN. What fish?

MR. FISHERMAN. I'm going out of my mind! The fish! The big fish! And the solid gold fish-hook. Here, wait — I'll show it to you. (*He searches his pockets. There is no fish-hook to be found.*) What did you do with that fish?

MRS. FISHERMAN. What fish?

MR. FISHERMAN. (*exasperated*) The fish! The fish I just brought home — the fish I didn't even know I'd caught!

MRS. FISHERMAN. Oh, that fish. Well, I put it on ice, of course.

MR. FISHERMAN. Go get it.

MRS. FISHERMAN. Go get what?

MR. FISHERMAN. The fish!

MRS. FISHERMAN. Which fish?

MR. FISHERMAN. (*holding on to his temper*) Will you please walk into the house . . . open the lid of the ice chest . . . and bring me the fish you put in it. Will you do that, Nancy?

MRS. FISHERMAN. (*deeply concerned*) Andy . . . are you all right?

MR. FISHERMAN. (*yells*) Go! (*She goes. She gets the fish out of the cooler.*)

MRS. TRIPPETT. Is everything all right out there, Nancy?

MRS. FISHERMAN. Oh . . . yes . . . Everything's fine. Andrew's lost his mind, that's all!

MRS. TRIPPETT. (*pantomimes tossing off a drink*) Been nipping, has he?

MRS. FISHERMAN. Not that I could smell — TELL! Excuse me. (*She races out and hands the fish to MR. FISH-ERMAN. He looks in its mouth. There is no fish-hook in it. He glares suspiciously at his wife.*)

MR. FISHERMAN. What did you do with it, Nancy?

MRS. FISHERMAN. With what?

MR. FISHERMAN. The hook! The gold hook! What did you do with it?

MRS. FISHERMAN. Gold?

MR. FISHERMAN. Yes, gold. Where is it?

MRS. FISHERMAN. I must have put it down some-where. I don't remember even seeing it. (*They hurry into the house and begin a frantic search.*)

MRS. TRIPPETT. Have you lost something?

MR. FISHERMAN. Yep.

MRS. FOLLOWELL. Can we help?

MRS. TRIPPETT. What is it? (*MR. FISHERMAN stops and stares at MRS. TRIPPETT for a long moment.*)

MR. FISHERMAN. (*excessively polite*) Mrs. Trippett. You didn't by any chance happen to see a gold fish-hook, did you. Say, lying right there on the table close to your hand.

MRS. TRIPPETT. Gold fish-hook! What fool would use a gold— I haven't seen *any* fish-hooks!

MR. FISHERMAN. You're quite sure of that, are you?

MRS. FISHERMAN. Andrew!

MRS. TRIPPETT. If you're implying, Mr. F.—

MR. FISHERMAN. I'm not implying anything—Mrs. T.

MRS. TRIPPETT. —that I took your fish-hook, you are sadly mistaken. Gold fish-hooks! What next?

MR. FISHERMAN. I brought a solid gold fish-hook into this house—

MRS. FISHERMAN. Andrew. You apologize this minute!

MR. FISHERMAN. I will not! (*to his wife*) Did I bring a gold fish-hook into this house or did I not?

MRS. FISHERMAN. You did not.

MR. FISHERMAN. Did you wish on that gold fish-hook for a little white cottage — or did you not?

MRS. FISHERMAN. I did not.

MR. FISHERMAN. And once you got it, pitched your two lady friends there out on their ear?

MRS. FISHERMAN. I did not.

MRS. TRIPPETT and MRS. FOLLOWELL. (*simultaneously*) She did not!

MR. FISHERMAN. And then . . . did you wish for a big stone castle, with lords and ladies prancing around as if they owned the world?

MRS. FISHERMAN. I did not.

MR. FISHERMAN. And that — not being good enough for you, oh, no! You had to be the Empress of all the world. Did you or did you not?

MRS. FISHERMAN. I did not.

MR. FISHERMAN. Even sicked your army on me because I didn't want to ask the fish for a blasted thing more —

MRS. FISHERMAN. Andy . . . you must have fallen asleep in that boiling sun — and dreamed all of this.

MR. FISHERMAN. I did not!

MRS. FISHERMAN. Well, you must have — because none of it happened.

MRS. FOLLOWELL. Dreams can be so real sometimes —

MR. FISHERMAN. (*to MRS. FOLLOWELL*) Stay out of this!

MRS. FISHERMAN. That may be — but you don't accuse other people of doing the things you cook up in your own dreams. Now Andrew, I want you to apologize. (*MR. FISHERMAN seems lost in a fog. Did he dream it?*)

MR. FISHERMAN. I dreamed it? No, I couldn't have. (*He's not sure.*)

MRS. FISHERMAN. (*waiting for his apology*) Andrew —

MR. FISHERMAN. Oh. Yeah. I apologize to all and sundry. Excuse me. (*He exits hurriedly, going off* R. *The ladies rise.*)

MRS. FISHERMAN. Where're you going? (*to the ladies*) I hope he's all right.

MRS. FOLLOWELL. Shouldn't we follow him?

MRS. TRIPPETT. Just what I was going to suggest.

(*All three of them leave the house and hurry off* R. *The lights dim out, and the curtain closes. MR. FISH-ERMAN enters* R., *carrying a powerful flashlight. He is searching for something. He cannot find it. At last, he stands* C. *and sings, quite sadly.*)

MR. FISHERMAN. (*sings*)
Fishie, fishie in the sea . . .
If you're real, come back to me—

(*He stops. He flashes the light into the audience, moving from one youngster to another.*)

Did you see my golden fish-hook? Did you? Did you? You saw the fish, didn't you? And the cottage? And the castle? They were real, weren't they? I didn't dream it, did I?

(*They will answer. Suddenly, he spots something shiny on the very lip of the stage—where FISH has put it. He picks it up. The spotlight comes on. The hook glistens and gleams in the light. He laughs triumphantly. The voices of the women are now heard off-stage. He hides the fish-hook in his pocket.*)

MRS. FISHERMAN. (*off*) Andrew! Where are you?

MRS. TRIPPETT and MRS. FOLLOWELL. Mr. Fisherman — yoo-hoo! Where are you?

MR. FISHERMAN. (*turns to face them*) Right here, ladies. Right here in front of you. Come on. Come on and join me.

MRS. FISHERMAN. (*enters*) Andy — I was so worried about you. Are you all right?

MR. FISHERMAN. Right as rain! Evening, ladies. (*MRS. TRIPPETT and MRS. FOLLOWELL are entering.*)

MRS. TRIPPETT. Oh, good! You found him!

MRS. FOLLOWELL. Oh, just let me catch my breath! Are you all right, Mr. Fisherman?

MR. FISHERMAN. Never been better. Everything's fine, ladies. What a glorious night! Let's all go home and see what's in that picnic basket! Let's go home . . . and see what we find.

MRS. FISHERMAN. Good, he's hungry! Long as a man's hungry, I know he's going to be fine! Shall we go, Andrew?

MR. FISHERMAN. (*bowing them out*) After you, dear ladies. (*The women exit, chattering happily. They do not look back. MR. FISHERMAN takes the fish-hook out of his pocket, holds it up in the air, displaying it. He tosses it over his head and catches it. Then he whispers to the audience.*) What shall I do with it? Should I throw it back into the sea? Or shall I keep it?

(*They will let him know. If they say keep it, he will rather gleefully put it back in his pocket. If they say, yes, throw it back into the sea — most unlikely — he will drop it into the pit. Either way, he exits*

R., *a most happy man. And the curtain goes out for company bows. Once the bows are over, MR. FISHERMAN signals for silence. He asks the audience if they would like to meet the actors. He tells them to stay in their seats — and then leads the company to the back of the theatre, where the youngsters can greet them — and receive little gold-fish crackers to munch on the way home.)*

THE END

PROP LIST

Fishing rod and reel
A large gold fish-hook
Hammer
Picnic basket, covered with red checked cloth
Rubber chicken
Long loaf of bread (unwrapped)
Duplicate red-checked table cloth (off R.)
Duplicate loaf of bread (off R.)
Duplicate rubber chicken (off R.)
2 plates, 2 coffee mugs, silverware
Fish, attachable to fishing line (in orchestra pit)
Flowers in a vase
Small ice cooler
Cot, chairs, table
Spreads for cot
Cloths for table
Large flashlight